T0123584

RAMBANTU

TEJASWI

Archway Publishing books may be ordered through booksellers or by contacting:

Archway Publishing
1663 Liberty Drive
Bloomington, IN 47403
www.archwaypublishing.com
844-669-3957

ISBN: 978-1-6657-5087-5 (sc)
ISBN: 978-1-6657-5088-2 (e)

Library of Congress Control Number: 2023919007

Print information available on the last page.

Archway Publishing rev. date: 10/10/2023

Contents

Prologue vii

Elephant 1

Sita Maha Lakshmi 54

Bantu 89

Elephant 111

Note from the Author 113

Prologue

Once upon a time, a cheerful little monkey was living an extravagant life in a deep forest. The Monkey is a bundle of force and joy. He jumps up and down, leaps from tree to tree, and runs fast and far. He wakes up to follow his beat.

Every trial he walks in, every tree he sits on, every river he swims, and every creature he spends time with becomes weary and wrestling.

He has many tricks and traps to make the most of the day. He knows, teases, and smiles at everyone. Although it feels tiresome because of his mischief, they cannot imagine a forest without him.

A Majestic celestial jungle tree "Amaravati" is rooting and growing amid the forest. The tree flowers bear fruit. Gods come to spend some time under the tree.

They found the little Monkey to be worthy of a blessing. They made a promise from the little Monkey that he would behave well and be a friend to all. In return, they gave him a gift of treasures and supernatural abilities.

Like always, the key to unfolding the blessings is kept a secret.

Gods await in eagerness to know how a little Monkey will grow up and find the key to unfold his blessings.

In the beautiful forest, eating papayas and mangoes, smelling Mongolia flowers, chasing butterflies, and drinking honey, the little Monkey has already grown up and has made many friends.

One fine day, while swimming in a river, he found a few jewelry pieces and saved them with him.

Every night the Monkey wonders what it means to have that jewelry with him.

A day came when an Avatar Purush, Prince Ram, walking with his brother, found the Monkey.

At first, Monkey cannot blink; the radiance of Prince Ram is such that it brings him to his knees. The Monkey can barely glimpse the man standing next to Prince Ram. He is lost in the eyes of Prince Ram with reverence and enchantment.

Prince Ram gently spoke, "Hanuman, my dear Monkey, I am Prince Ram; this is my brother, Lakshman. We are walking in the forest, searching for my beloved wife."

"This beautiful forest is receiving us from star to star, tree to tree, flower to flower, word to word, bird to bird, and eventually leading to you. Have you seen my beloved wife?"

The Monkey, vividly lost in his thought, quickly went, and brought the jewelry from his cave.

He gave it to Prince Ram and said, "I found them in the river. I haven't seen anyone."

Prince Ram knelt on the ground, tearing up a little, while patting the head of the Monkey, and said to him, "This is my beloved wife Sita's jewelry."

"Myself, my beloved wife, and my dearest brother have been living in the forest for a while now. With her by my side, this beautiful forest was my sanctuary. We brothers went on a quest, and she was lost in the wilderness by the time of our return."

"I want to bring her back home. I want to look into her eyes once again to witness the unconditional love for myself."

Touch by the love Prince Ram has for his beloved wife, the Monkey says: "Lotus eyes, weep not, I am a friend of all."

"I have many friends, and we all are your friends; we will walk, fly, swim, as you wish, and find your beloved for you. We can and we will."

The gods are now very cheerful and enthusiastic about the journey forward. Prince Ram has finally found the key to unfolding the Monkey's treasures and supernatural abilities with his love for his beloved wife. The monkey became Prince Ram's Bantu.

Avatar Purush: The one who appears to restore order.

Bantu: A beloved Bond servant.

Elephant

I have told this story many times and lost count of it. I even broke my tusk to write this story on a mountain. You might be living far away from where I am. I might sound like, "Phawooo! Phawoooo!"

It takes a great deal of energy to narrate a story. I must trumpet, rumble, roar, do little squeaks, flap my ears in between, and if I am soaking in a bath, I sound like bubbling. Be aware regardless of the sounds I make, one can only listen to them in their sounds. In your world, they call it a language.

Let's begin with the story...

I am the first one to wake up in my territory. I must wake everyone up with a trumpet. It is duty, pride, and something I heartfully love. Because I get to invite Sun into our world.

One beautiful spring day in the land of the rising Sun. I stood on top of a magnificent golden mountain to invite the Sun.

Today as I stood in front of a golden hue sky, before the Sun, came a wave of Sun flares, closer to my world and my eyes. At first, I thought to roar, but I couldn't squeak a little.

As it came closer, looking a lot less like a Sun flare and more like a Monkey spinning through the waves of the Sun.

A monkey from another world, a wanderer of the skies, a celestial being.

The little Monkey drops and lands right in front of my feet. Looks beautiful, serene, simple, and at ease.

The gold complexion, self-illuminating, and with an effortless, relaxing posture.

Dusting off the burnt orange dust and blowing off the flames, it quickly says, "Hi."

Before I could say or ask something, it did a somersault and already took a crawl over my trunk and sat on my head.

"It's time for a new day; welcome the Sun, my friend." speaking with a lovely, gentle voice.

It is a bit scary, but the old bear came just in time to fill me up with some secrets of the beyond.

"Don't fear this little celestial wanderer. He indeed arrives from beyond."

"Beyond?"

Yes, this little monkey serves the Viswam, the creation.

Viswam: Universe, Cosmos, everything that is in creation.

He and his commander dive into the Viswam to travel and explore the world within the creation.

The star paths always take them separately and reunite them by purpose. They reunite to eat, play, relax, and stay together for the world's benefit.

They share deep friendship; they travel and explore many worlds together, playing in stardust, atoms, and elements.

The chief has a purpose: To benefit the worlds inside the creation. Benefit the world with welfare, happiness, and prosperity.

They call their mission "Loka Kalyanam."

The little monkey's mission is to align and be in momentum with his master's mission.

Like a child to his father, like a fellow traveler, like a savior, like a wise monk, like a dear friend, he finds his way back to his master.

Loka Kalyanam: For the highest good and harmony of the world.

"Yes, my commander, my chief, my dearest friend, my prince, is an avid adventurer, curious, and very kind." the Monkey says beaming with pride.

"I get to reunite and bond with him in every element of the creation. All elements, stars, waves, and paths reach one beyond all worlds."

"Why are you here again?" I asked.

"To live a quiet life, to be your friend in the meantime, to play with you, to be happy with you, that's all I do until the paths of the stars unfold to give me another chance to meet my chief, my prince, my friend, to see him, as many times as I can, and be one with him."

"In a few moments, the monkey forgets all his superpowers." said the old bear.

"Superpowers?"

Yes, he has eight superpowers. He will forget all of them.

1. He can shrink to the size of a tiny little bee.
2. He can grow into a size, as big as a Mountain.
3. He can look like a little Monkey but weigh heavier than a mountain.
4. He can even feel as light as a feather.
5. He can easily win and obtain anything.
6. If anyone desires something, he will fulfill them.
7. He can create for us; with bare hands, he creates dust, stardust, fire, flame, water, and milk. He can clap and create magic.
8. He can even control us. Everyone likes him, and everyone trusts him.

Well, it's time for honey tasting; I will have to go, said the old bear waving goodbye and leaving us with each other.

"Except for the memories with my chief, my precious friend, everything else goes away, but memories stay, some good, some sad; they dwell in my heart as a compass. Always fills me up with quietness and a longing to meet him again." said the monkey looking at the old bear walking away.

It took a few glances, a little walk, and a bath soaking in the pool for the little monkey to be one of us and my dearest friend. That's all.

He has many stories to say and many names to call, but he goes easy with Bantu.

Bantu, the monkey, came to live a tranquil life with us on the mountain. He became a friend of all. Wherever he goes, by the end of the day, just before the sky shows up with stars, he returns to his home.

Everyone in the mountain, and the mountain waits for him to return home. Before he sleeps, he tells us all one good story, and the entire mountain listens to him.

All his stories are the same; they all start with my chief and I once...

We discovered a pathway into the world of the Sun.

We once painted a moon, created rings around the planet, fueled vitality into the trees.

We play in the rivers, float across the skies, and dive into many oceans.

We once met a specimen on a faraway land. The species has a problem; whenever or whomever they touch, embrace, or hold, they burn and vanish. My master found them a medicine; He has shown them how to hold on to each other without burning.

We once saw a species preparing to vanish and become extinct from one planet due to a lack of resources and space; we gave them advice to stay on the same planet as invisible creatures and access plenty of hidden resources from the same world.

The star's paths divide our paths for a purpose. In the meantime, I wait for the paths to unfold. So, I get to meet my prince again.

"You met him many times already; why do you want to meet him again?" I ask.

"He makes me feel at home. With my friend, with him by my side, it is easy to play, eat more, eat very little, and eat nothing. It is easy to fly, swim, dance, climb, jump, and stay still; more than anything, it is easy to say Yes to him for any journey, crossover, or adventure. He is a true friend of mine. And to look into his benevolent eyes one more time or just to wait for him to arrive, I must be very fortunate."

"To watch the Sunrise from this magnificent golden mountain is a grand spectacle; with you by my side, every day is a good day."

Bantu says kind words in the early hours of the day. Also, he is excellent at picking the right spots to watch the Sunrise.

I play trumpet, trumpet, and trumpet. Bantu stretches his every bone, limb, and tail. He massages his face and rubs his stomach and chest. Taps his body to wake up.

Once we are done soaking in golden hour hue brilliance. He drops into the pool to douse with his fellow monkey friends, and I bathe with my folks.

Morning baths are fun; we are half awake, yawning, floating, gliding, and listening to the birds.

The Monkeys sit in groups to groom each other in the Sunshine. Setting hair in place, rubbing fragrances on the skin, removing dust, massaging their eyes, and rubbing their hands and feet as they prepare for the day.

But I am an elephant; I get dirty and soak in the river. Then I get to roll and be muddier, then I run back into the water, and now I need more mud, need more river.

The deer, elk, goats, and a group of white horses are already up and running in the glory of raising the Sun. Birds sing, Bears quietly look for the honey, and I prepare for the walk. The mountain feels very uplifting at this early hour of the day.

Jumping, squealing, whistling, from tree to tree, branch to branch, throwing some nuts at the rabbits and squirrels. Bending branches to make deer eat hassle-free. Leaping onto my back, Bantu casually hangs around with me during my walk.

In the beginning, he inquires me, do you see the Mountain standing next to our Mountain? I say, "No."

He then asks the lion, parrot, and squirrel, and everyone says, "No."

A few days later, He began to ask, "I am going to eat some fresh fruit on the other Mountain; anyone wants to join?" We at the territory are still persistent with our answer.

Bantu starts playing tricks to entertain us and mostly to take us on the trail to the Invisible Mountain. He brings flowers, nuts, honey, fruits, and fragrances and says, "I got it from the invisible Mountain right next to us; it is bountiful and beautiful."

A little ant, a parrot, and a bee took their first steps and sat in turns on the shoulders of our friend Bantu.

Ant made it midway.
Parrot made it only a few steps.
A bee could make it only one step.

He brought them back without forcing them further.

We at the Mountain have always had many questions for Bantu.

"Why can't we see it?" I ask.

"Well, it is a treasure; you must have a little faith and trust to see it.", says Bantu.

"I never saw an ocean before. Does the invisible Mountain stay next to an ocean?", Asks a rabbit.

"Yes, you can see an ocean next to the mountain.", says Bantu.

"Well, then, get us the conch." Says the rabbit.

He went and got us back a little blue conch.

The rabbit quickly got hold of the conch and looked into my eyes.

An invisible Mountain stands next to the Mountain we live in; it is beautiful, bountiful, a paradise, a treasure; we don't see it, but now we know it because we have faith in this star voyager. He is one of us. It's tempting and exciting to know that our world is expanding, and we have more space and harmony.

"But only if we could see it," I whispered in his ears.

Tired, desperate, and frustrated. Bantu took the conch shell from the hands of the rabbit, pulled a thread from his tail, made it into a necklace, and tied it around his neck.

It is a little painful; I can see a tear dropping from his eyes. He then runs to the cliff of the Mountain, leaning back a little, standing up, then folding forward smoothly, offering a Namaste to the Sun; he lunges forward with his left foot, opening his chest and arms, into the air for a Sun spin.

It is his anger that took him a little further. It usually takes Sunrise to Sunset for him to come back. But for now, it took him more than that. He must have gone further, crossing many worlds already.

And we were curious to know if we had to wait for him.

"He is one of us; he will return to us." said the Owl.

"I will keep watching; you all go back to sleep."

It took so much spirit for me to wake up the next day, I didn't want to open my eyes, but I did; I didn't want to walk, but I took one step at a time; little Crow kept my company, and there we stood watching the Sunrise, a show of grandeur, beholding my spirit, I trumpet; trumpet; trumpet...

In the world of Sanjeevani, life is very fulfilling.

Layer by layer, decking up with little cottages, flowers, fruits, vegetable gardens, and flowing rivers, all aligning to be a lotus flower.

For the outsiders, it is just a wild rose of a world beloved by butterflies and sky wanderers. If you are fortunate enough to find and enter the island of the world, you enter paradise.

Bouncing up and down, jumping up in the air, stretching his tail, the monkey somehow found an elevation and a view to see the entire world of Sanjeevani, and it is just a flower, a wild rose.

Sanjeevani: A world of paradise with beautiful flowers, herbs, bountiful vegetation, beautiful and delicate natives, one Sun, and two moons.

The Sun spin always makes him hungry, so he searches for food. He finds a Mango tree and jumps on it with force.

Touching, smelling, squeezing, and then tasting. Monkey ate all the sweet mangoes, left half-eaten sour ones to the parrots, and longingly looked at the unripe fruits.

The mischief jumping and teasing every bird around brought the leaves, branches, flowers, and twigs to lay waste on the grass. The Mango tree is tired and worn out already.

The Monkey's eyes are now quickly relaxing into a nap. The bees are helping him with light scratching here and there, his tail gently coiling around a branch, and he safely sleeps like a baby.

Right next to the field of wild roses, Sita is sleeping. The deer came running in the Sun's golden rays, kissing her feet and cheeks. She gently pulls them into a cuddle while finding ways and fighting her spirit to take her back to restful sleep.

It's a summer day, and the deer sets free from her cuddle and runs up to the hills, waking Sita to take her to the trial barefoot.

Comforting in a Yellow and white garments, hair tied in a half bun with a gold accessory, and a long pearl necklace, she wore something like this almost every day.

The shepherd stood lost in directions and found his distractions; the herd of sheep, in a hurry, decides to follow Sita onto the trial.

It is a very long hike, but she does it every day to eat fresh fruit in the early hours.

Her father saves her the clean, sweet, and delicious Mangoes. Her Mom offers her freshly squeezed fruit juice. She sometimes gets lucky finding the most delightful fruit all by herself. On the days she couldn't, she quietly returned home to eat the fruit from home.

Between the chaos of Sheep looping around her and fawns kissing and snuggling her feet, she stood staring at the Mango tree with wonder, innocence, and bewilderment.

The shepherd came looking and calling for the sheep, and the herd found their way back to their Master.

While the deer were quietly eating at her feet, she stood staring at the Mango tree, hanging in there after handling a storm; Summer could not take the blame for it, but a monkey indeed must.

We call her a beloved, for humans let's call her Sita, and the monkey's name is Bantu.

I am an Elephant, and I care a little less about having a name, but the important thing here is you are listening to this story because I am telling you one.

Bantu put on a charming smile, his head tilting side to side and eyes conveniently darting into Sita's eyes. Of course, he is very aware of wrecking up a mango tree and quickly guesses by looking at her face that Sita is very upset about it.

Bantu, the monkey, is a friend of all; to make a friend, he jumps, cartwheels, and lands next to her feet. Driving the deer away, he upsets her again. He then slowly offers her the conch.

Sita hesitantly but quietly picks up the conch and instinctively listens to it.

As soon as she brings it to her ears, music from the conch starts to play out loud; it's a beautiful melody of drums.

Bantu grabs it and hears it.

He listens to a simple and endearing voice calling Bantu.

Sita asks, "Bantu?"

"It's my name." He confirms.

"Who is calling?" asks Sita.

"My master, chief, commander, dearest friend..." says Bantu.

"Calling me from the farthest world..." says Bantu.

Bantu broke into happy tears, melting his own heart and Sita's.

Sita quickly remembers something. "A monkey and his chief on a mission?"

Bantu Nods.

"So, this is a story my mother tells me every night to help me sleep and dream sweet dreams," says Sita.

"What did she say?" asks Bantu.

"Many stories, many of them," says Sita.

She told me you once wrote all your adventures with your chief on a stone with your nails until he found his way back to you. Your blood became a river and Moon drops cleansed it into pure water river.

You both have won battles, saved worlds, built bridges across, laid trials to multiple universes and realms, and lifted heavy mountains, planets, and distant stars.

My mother also told me that you both share an irreplaceable bond promising eternity, not for a lifetime, but forever.

She also told me you both return to each other in every world, element, and beyond.

She also told me that you will never go to any land that your master, your chief, hasn't gone before.

"Yes." Bantu nodded with a smile.

"If you are here, it must mean he has been here too," says Sita.

"A definite yes," confirms Bantu.

"So, how long have we been away from each other?" asks Sita.

"When will you meet him again?" asks Sita.

My mother told me, you once stood as a stone mountain until your master landed his feet on you.

"Yes," confirms Bantu.

It's been a while; it feels like an epoch already. But it feels like we are getting closer to each other.

"So, how are you finding him now?" asks Sita.

"Looks like you already helped me to recover a treasure," says Bantu.

"A treasure?"

"Yes, the conch."

Listen to his voice; Bantu stretches his hands to meet Sita's ears.

Sita hears a gentle, warm, familiar, and simple voice saying, "Aye."

Bantu cannot contain his happiness; he hops, bounces, and moves to dance.

Hoping on the sides, bouncing up and down, laughing out loud, hands on his knees, closing his fists to punch and then clapping his hands in the air, giving himself a warm hug, swinging, crossing his hands in the air.

Sita stares at him first, then starts to follow his steps, bounces up and down, hops in circles, closes her fist to punch Bantu's fists, claps hands with Bantu's palms, hugs herself warmly, and then swings, crossing her hands in the air.

They are friends already. They both lay on the grass to rest and breathe the air.

This is a treasure; you have just helped me to recover.

I am one step closer to meeting my Prince, my master.

"I thought the invisible mountain is the treasure, looks like it is somebody's desire, but this conch is the treasure."

"Bantu, what is a treasure?" asks Sita.

"A treasure is anything that finds its value. Like this conch, it is just a conch I grabbed from the ocean. The moment it brought a message from my master, it became a treasure for me."

"Sometimes the value lasts forever, sometimes just for a moment."

"This conch gave me an assurance of protection, support, and encouragement to follow the path without fear."

He picked the conch and tied it back as a necklace. Rolling up his spine at ease, Bantu says,

"I have to get back."

"Where are you going?"

"Maybe recover another treasure."

"Oh."

Bantu walks a little ahead and turns around.

"Will you join me?"

Sita looks at him with a question of concern and safety.

Bantu quickly assures.

"I will bring you back home safely".

Sita looks at him and says, "Yes."

"But I have to return home safely, to my beloved parents."

Bantu leans into assure "I promise."

Bantu raises his chest, opens his arms, and then blows the conch.

All the Deer's quietly gather around Sita. They quietly came to see her go to another world. While one deer kisses her feet, Sita, lovingly patting its head, gets ready for the journey.

Out of thin air, a bundle of petals slowly wraps her into sleep.

They lift her, she floats across, and Bantu escorts her, doing his Sun spin.

She briefly, quietly took a nap to arrive.

Landing is easy too, as easy as petals dropping from a flower and her feet are on the Golden Mountain.

I saw both Bantu and Sita landing and running toward me.

I did the roar, making sure everyone gathered around.

Bantu first came and bowed to me.

Sita also bent her chin, quickly looking into my eyes, to please and smile. Trying to be familiar.

As an apology, Bantu reached out to his bum and kept punching himself, then he did the sit-ups until I flapped my ears and squeaked a little.

If I forgive him, everyone around will forgive him.

So, I said, "Bantu, we are all a little taken aback; you can go anytime, anywhere, and choose not to come again, not now or forever."

"Next time, if you choose to go, let me know; let us all know. So, that we don't wait for you to come back." I quietly said.

Bantu bowed his head down and brought his hands to his heart.

"I came here from far away galaxy to not just be as a visitor, but to be one of you, to benefit you, to add to your happiness, welfare, and prosperity."

"But we cannot see the mountain; we cannot see the bridge." said the eagle flying across the gathering.

Sita quickly came closer to Bantu. To assure him that he is not standing alone.

Bantu said, "If I came here, there is some treasure I must recover, maybe not the Mountain, it could be just a desire, but something other than that. Holding his conch in a tight clasp."

I asked everyone to disperse, and I looked down to the Mountain. I see nothing, no ocean, no land, no space.

In this world, the only place we can survive is this beautiful Mountain. We got only this Mountain to call home.

Strangely an entire world for a mountain, as if overnight someone picked up a mountain and brought us into this world while we were all asleep, and we forgot where we came from.

We have everything here under this sky, and everything we have is on this lovely Mountain.

I always dreamt of this world to be more than a Mountain. It's my desire. But for now, this is all I can see; this is all we have got. A graceful Mountain standing in solitude with our wilderness and making us feel at home.

While every one of us left them casually. Sita and Bantu slowly first and then, with happy laughter, starts to run.

Every one of us simply ignored to follow, but we are all aware of their words and trials.

As long as we live on this Mountain, we all are completely aware of everything that happens here. We all share a connection.

Bantu and Sita ran across the mountain to reach the milk pond.

The milk pond is in a little quiet corner. Most of us avoid the trial to the path of the milk pond. For one simple reason, like everything else in this world, that little milk pond is a mystery.

Snow white elephants, Moonstones, White horses, Swans, and White owls live around the pond.

Except for them, none of us could cross or drink from the milk pond; even the Sun, in its full glory, will only look like a Moon.

Sita got a glimpse of the elegance and grace of the snow-white elephants. She saw the swans gliding in the pond and white horses running free.

Bantu knelt on his knees, pleading for the snow-white elephant to help him cross the milk pond.

Iravatha, a snow-white elephant bubbling with a deep sigh, stood up. Bantu took a crawl over the trunk, sat on the back, and they both looked at Sita.

Surprised by the scenic serenity around her, Sita stood gently looking into the eyes of the Iravatha trying to please. Iravatha turns away and takes the Monkey across the milk pond to the other side.

Bantu putting his hands on his head, looks very disappointed that the Iravatha didn't offer Sita a ride.

"I did offer her a ride; she was just staring at me." says Iravatha.

"She is shy," Monkey said very secretly.

"Not my problem." sighs Iravatha.

Iravatha: One amongst a pair of snow-white elephants.

While Bantu looks stuck and upset across the milk pond. Sita quickly steps onto the Moonstone and takes a sail effortlessly.

Bantu made gestures of celebration. Everyone in the mountain and all the monkey crew gather to watch Sita cross the milk pond.

She simply sat on the Moonstone with a bit of poise while giving a winning smile to Iravatha and sailing the pond.

All the Monkeys climbed the trees enthusiastically, and one clever Monkey took a quick look and guessed; this sail has something to do with the pearl necklace around her neck.

He immediately jumped onto Sita, grabbed the pearl necklace, and ran off. The Moonstone lost its balance, dropping Sita into the milk pond.

Bantu whistles for help in a hurry. A few monkeys quickly went to get the Pearl necklace back. The rest found as many moonstones as possible to throw into the milk pond.

Bantu went back to Iravatha to snuggle his trunk and plea for help. Iravatha, pulling back, gave a strike on Bantus Bum with his long trunk, denying any service.

Iravatha also gave a warning not to disturb him again with his body language, eyes, and tone.

Frowning and drowning in fear, Sita couldn't find a way to swim, float or stay still. The little tortoise came flipping around her, bringing her in a direction and making her breathe easily. Sita recovering to flow a little follows up with the little turtle, met the entire marine family in the milk pond.

The fishes in the milk pond slowly came to orbit around Sita. Leaving the bubbles slowly, Sita found a way to ease and relax by diving into the pond and staring back at the lovely fishes.

The big fish said, "Dear, this is a milk pond. To enter this pond, you must be as pure as white, but you recklessly have mud all over your body and are wearing something yellow."

"Now clean your body and the pond first," commanded the big fish.

Sita, dropping and rolling herself to touch the pond's ground, starts to wipe off the mud on her body.

The little fish came to assist her in cleaning the mud across the milk pond, and some were generous enough to scrub the dirt off her skin. Together they have made a mud hill.

The big fish is still upset.

But before it could say anything, everyone saw a little flower blooming up from the little mud hill.

A Little pink flower with a green stem and mud roots is barely born.

With a lushing brightness, the Sun's rays found their way to the deep end of the milk pond. Illuminating and nurturing the little bud, every fish saw the flower growing in the Sunshine.

The little flower gently woke up and immediately sucked Sita into the center. All the fish gather around and begin to circle around Sita.

Sita sits inside the flower.

"Is it going to eat her?" asks the big fish.

"No," said Sita.

Little by little, Sita found a way to relax in the flower. The more she found a way to relax, the easier it got for the flower to lift her to the surface of the milk pond.

Sita's appearance brought Sun to bring a brightness of a thousand Suns to celebrate a flower blossom.

The first ever pink flower grown in the milk pond. All the monkeys, fishes, birds, animals, and worms are vigilant, cheerful, clapping, and singing.

"She is here for the good of all."

Under the Sun, petal by petal, thousand petals, unwrapping to blossom, a flower.

In her yellow dress, Sita sat in the center of the flower, shining, and illuminating with the golden glow of the Sun's rays.

Once the flower was in full blossom, Sita stood on her feet, in the center of the flower, and did a little twirl.

The monkeys kept jumping down from one tree, cartwheeling, and crawling to the next tree to celebrate.

Butterflies of all colors came to flutter around Sita. Fish jumping out of water, Swans came together to glide into dance, and the Sun was showering her with golden rays. Iravatha ran to shower Sita with milk.

Slowly sailing on a flower, Sita met Bantu.

Bantu whispers, "The lotus flower is a treasure."

"How?" Ask Sita.

"By being who you are, you inspire others to be who they are."

"Any flower, any time, any person, or any place, word, or song, that helps you, inspires you, and allows you to be who you are is a Treasure."

Look at the Sun; it is shining, like it always does, without pretending to be a Moon.

Watching pink lotus bloom and blossom in a milk pond is inspiring. Making you feel you can be who you are.

Look at all of them; they celebrate just because this moment encourages them to be who they are.

Sita, Bantu, and everyone stood looking at the beauty of the giant lotus flower showering in the Sun's golden rays and floating across the milk pond. The swans are gliding and dancing.

Yeilding myself a little low to pick Sita and Bantu, I took them up to the top of the mountain.

Little Whispers, claps, and happiness as if we are ready to invite change and something new.

I gave that look to my friend, Bantu. "Yes, we are all ready for change and willing to see the invisible mountain and take this one step forward."

Bantu took a flight back and forth to Invisible Mountain. We all kept cheering and clapping for him. He knelt on the ground and asked Sita.

"There is a mountain over there; it is visible for the ones willing to trust; it is bountiful, beautiful, it is what it is if you trust it, they will all have it with you, the happiness of finding something new, expansion of their own little world. I don't want to say too many words. Will you walk with me step by step?"

Sita obviously couldn't say No but didn't know how to say Yes.

She stood at the end of the cliff, looking at all of us. I, for courtesy, came forward and told her, "You don't have to do it if you are not ready. We are all happy with what we already have."

However, the silly monkey steps into the air, creating an ice crystal out of thin air. Then he took another step; another ice crystal took form.

Sita quickly puts her feet on the ice crystal; however, it drops into the air, and she pulls her feet back on the ground.

Sita jerked a little and stood staring into Bantu's eyes.

Bantu told her, "If you choose to come, you must come by yourself, creating your own trial, you're your own path."

"Oh"

Every one of us went a little closer to the cliff of the mountain as Sita put her foot forward.

Our hearts became stiff and cold when she put her foot forward into the air.

Sita indeed has enough trust to take the other foot into the air just by looking into the eyes of the Bantu.

A little lotus flower blossoms out of the air to hold her safe and steady, and then, with happiness, she takes tiny little steps and starts to run back and forth.

Our hearts are easy, open, free, and happy.

Every step of hers was steady and safe as the flowers kept blooming, leaving a trail of a flower garden all the way.

She returned to us, saying, "Trust in me; there is a Mountain there, beautiful and bountiful."

A wave of happiness surrounded us, and Bantu asked, "Who will go next?"

"I will," said the little squirrel.

We all laughed, and I advised her to wait a little.

The Tiger said, "I will go First."

Yes, we all approve; it takes courage and strength to do this first, and who is better than a Tiger.

With our approval, he went forward, took a few steps, and found himself walking on a bed of rocks.

The celebrations began; We made music out of rocks, our voices sang hymns for the hour, the little squirrel left a trail of tree branches, ants left a mud trail, and rabbits left a trail of bushes.

It is the turn of the little fox, walking eloquently and leaving a fragile blade of grass trial.

Looking at the thin glass blade trial, everyone started to laugh, and with embarrassment, the little fox jumped onto the trail of rocks the Tiger left behind.

As soon as the little fox stepped onto the rock, it lost balance, and the little fox was set for a fall.

Until then, I was just sitting and cheering, and within a gasp of a breath, I stood and took the leap, walking, running, to catch him from the fall.

Bantu came to into the moment, and I ran to cuddle. We caught him halfway, and the little fox, with fear, held on to me, leaning on my back, and I took him forward.

Cheers, claps, a wave of excitement, and enthusiasm, as I stepped forward and stood on the new Mountain.

What I left behind is not a trial but a bridge between two mountains. A way is found and laid to the invisible Mountain. The Mountain is no longer hidden; Everyone can see it; not the ones who trusted enough to take a few steps towards it but those still standing on the other side. It didn't feel like I was creating a path at all, but it was unfolding itself, and I am just moving forward.

As they say, it is true; if we can see something clearly, there is already a path to take us there.

The herd of Lions silently and leisurely walked on the bridge leading the birds and the animals to the other side.

I stood looking proud into the eyes of my dearest friend Bantu with an apology and gratitude.

A terrain of golden mountains reflecting the vastness of our world. Our sky got widened. A bountiful and beautiful golden mountain amid a blue ocean, under a beautiful sky.

Monkeys went crazy; they ran on the bridge, found honey, and got drunk. All the wildlife kept running across the bridge.

They picked flowers, turmeric, honey, herbs, fruit, flower, and tree milk. Bathing, singing, exploring, dancing, laughing, crying, eating, drinking, hugging, and celebrating.

"And this is a land of your own, someone's desire, a monument of abundance standing amid the vastness of blue ocean, under vast sky of glowing light. You all found it by courage and by your ability to trust in each other. Courage to make your own path and leading others with compassion will always expand your world into the realms of infinite vastness." Bantu gave a short speech.

It is the happiest day of my life. I took a very slow walk, listening to the crowd, and finding way down to the foot of the Mountain, sat under a waterfall, to enjoy myself with a little shower and happy dance. Afterall, I build a terrain.

How great of me.

Turns out I wasn't alone here; somebody else was gently sleeping, lazily floating, and harshly alive.

The crocodile attack is direct and desperate. It drowned me out of my power, and I shouted for help.

I knew the rest couldn't hear my loud shrills as they were all celebrating, but I shouted anyway.

I am here alone, almost powerless as prey to this desperate danger. I could leave life any moment; my blood was flowing into the river, my voice was almost shaking and reaching back to me with low echoes of mountains, and I was losing consciousness. Fighting with my spirit, I made sounds, small, loud, voiceless, pulling myself back and fighting with the crocodile as much as I could, and I willingly stood fighting as long as

I could without expecting anything else; I simply put up with a fight until I forgot that I am fighting the crocodile and realized I am just fighting.

Sita, and Bantu came running. Bantu jumped onto the crocodile and looked completely helplessly. He didn't know how to fight it.

Sita commanded him. "**Bantu become heavier than a Mountain.**"

Bantu simply obeyed and realized he could look like a little monkey and weigh like a Mountain. One of his superpowers. The crocodile let lose my leg and slide smoothly into the river.

"Why did you just let him go?" Asks Sita.

"Because he is a treasure, too," replies Bantu.

"How?" Asks Sita.

"A treasure will force you to stand in your own true power. It reminds you of your superpower; standing in your true power drives any danger away."

The old bear gave me medicine, and I was ready to rest and relax by Sunset.

"It's time for me to return home," said Sita.

We all are a little moved; we don't want her to go; of course, I can see Bantu, and he feels like he doesn't want her to let go yet.

So, first, I took a few steps toward Bantu and asked, "Go ahead and drop her home safely."

Bantu looked at me very upset, and I said, "Sita had to go home to her parents."

Bantu inquired whether we found her the pearl necklace.

"Yes," they said, and one monkey gave him the pearl necklace.

Bantu went and dropped the pearl necklace into her hands.

Sita took it and wore it back around her neck and spoke.

"It's time to go home; take me back; the Sun is about to set."

But the naughty monkey can't stop himself from nagging. Bantu rolled in mud, cried, and convinced her to stay here for just tonight.

Can't you see this journey is not just mine but yours too.

Bantu holding back his tears, blurts out every possible sound he can make to deliver a fine speech.

"You helped me to recover the message of encouragement in the conch. You made us realize by being who we are, we can have everything and even can sail in the milk pond. You led us by courage and made us trust each other by taking that one step forward by trusting a friend in me and brought everyone to this beautiful and bountiful Mountain, and in the hour of danger, you made us realize our superpower."

Being her kind self and understanding, it was hard for Bantu to let go and say goodbye. Sita politely said "Every journey ends somewhere; maybe this is the end of my chapter"

"This journey is as much as your journey as much as mine. We are in this together; I feel it is your journey than mine." Said Bantu.

"I am very sure if you give me that pearl necklace, it will become a treasure too."

"Only you can recognize treasures for me; only you can," said Bantu with teary eyes.

Then he ran, crawled, climbed the tallest tree, and sat there for a while.

"You promised me that you would take me home." Called Sita.

We all looked at him, waiting for him to stop nagging. He isn't ready for Sita to let go.

I commanded the other monkeys to get him. The rest of them went behind him, and no one could catch him.

Sita felt restless and said, "Well, I will figure out a way myself."

She walked and wept, and we all followed her.

"Is there a mango tree here?" asked Sita.

I have shown her the way.

Sita went there, and there he was, Bantu almost looking like he knew where she would arrive.

Bantu, "I want to go home; fulfill your promise, my desire because only you can fulfill this desire for me commanded Sita."

He kept his hands towards the Sunset, and a little Sun flare came into his palms. He gave it to Sita, "Now draw a flower, and it will take you home."

Sita receives the flame and draws a flower under the mango tree.

The flame flower is suddenly ready to take flight. Sita sat in the middle, and she went home.

It wasn't long since she left the mango tree; The shepherd just took the sheep, the parrots were still eating the half-eaten fruits, the deer were still feeding on the grass, and the flute was still playing in the early hour of the day.

The rest of the day is unusually dull. Sita felt she had seen herself in extraordinary and enchanting circumstances. The most beautiful part of the journey was that she trusted herself with everything that came her way. It remains a beautiful secret in her heart.

Having a family and loving them dearly is more enchanting to her than any magical ride. She is okay to be who she is rather than who she can ever be. Seeing her family made her feel safe. Hugging her father, kissing her mother, and playing with her brother brought solace to her.

Bantu, however, felt a little upset. He didn't tell any stories that night. But the following day, he is up and ready. Picking up the right spot for the Sun gaze, bathing in the pool, grooming with his monkey friends, and then joining me on my Morning walk and playing in the waterfall shower with me.

He relentlessly found ways to live, laugh, be friends, and play with us. He is there with us all day, every day.

He isn't searching, he isn't looking, or even traveling. He is one with us, like one of us, and he is okay with it.

However, it made us realize it was time for him to go away.

After a few discussions and long deep thoughts for many days, I, and the old Bear, came to a conclusion. Bantu must take off from here. I want to give him directions. I want to free him from his burden of being one of us; after all, he will always be a wanderer.

We held a gathering, we had some plays, sharing stories, singing songs, kicking, and pulling each other in tease, and then I took the stage, looking into my friend's eyes, and said, "Bantu, you have truly been one of us, brought us happiness, prosperity, and harmony, Thank you."

"It's time for you to go."

"Where?" He asked, choking a little.

"Take your next step."

"How?"

"Go and live with Sita..."

"Sita chose her family. She decides to stay with them, not own this journey, and I don't want to force her to be or do something she is unwilling to", said Bantu.

"Yes, Sita chose her family because she knew and trusted them all her life. Don't you think she will go to any place her family takes her to?

"She will."

"So now Go to her, stay with her, play with her, be her friend, and be her family."

"If you make her feel what her family makes her feel, if Sita knows she can trust you as family, she will be whatever you want her to be and do whatever you want her to do."

"But this isn't about me; this is about her; it is her journey."

"You are supposed to be her friend, a guide."

"Sita came to recover the treasures because she kept her faith in your story; this is not just about her journey. It is yours too."

I said to Bantu, "Everyone in the mountain now believes you are one of us; you can go wherever you want; we will be okay because everyone here trusts we will be okay; when we are not okay, we know you will know, and you will come to rescue because we trust you; you are one of us, you are family."

And she needs someone to trust her like we trust you; Sita earned it by keeping her trust in you first, and now you must have faith in her.

Bantu understood it; He came and hugged me and slept that night right next to me. And yes, he told us a story.

After the Sun rises. All the monkeys, lions, birds, tigers, elephants, squirrels, deer, and elks stood in the gathering.

The old bear and I stood to command him for a Sun spin. Birds sang farewell, I put on the trumpet show, and the wise old bear read the commandments for a Sun spin, and before that, we all said one last goodbye.

As we kept cheering, the old bear announced the twelve steps of the Sun spin.

1. Offer Namaste to the Sun, stand on your feet, and embrace the eternal giver with all your heart.
2. Raise your hands and arms, lean back, align your toes to your head, bring your hands close to your ears, stretch your spine, and take a deep breath. Open your heart to the eternal force of the Sun, who is ever-present.
3. Keep your spine erect, relax, roll forward, and release your breath. Surrender to the force.
4. Incline up, lunge with the left leg forward, take flight, and breathe in. Raise up to the Sun's glory. Let go of everything and leave all your worries.
5. Once up and flying, relax and stretch back your left leg and be straight, erect, and breathe out. Be consistent in your nature. Let the self-luminous essence of the Sun help you find balance.
6. Adjust your knees, hands, chin, chest, and feet; adjust the size and weight, to align with the motion of the Sun, grounding, and breathing in.

7. Tuck your toes, push forward in force with your navel raised to your chest, and let the Sun guide you in the right direction, destination, and timing. Relax and simply float at your pace.
8. Once you see the destination, raise your hips, lower your chest, and stretch to come down while adjusting size and weight and taking a deep breath. Pledge to be the benefit of others on the land.
9. Put your right foot forward to lunge on the land and ease out your breath. Find your ground; find your balance.
10. Bring back the left foot forward, bring the knees together, bend to touch your feet, and ease out on breathing out. Be humble.
11. Roll the spine up, peel off dust from your spine, align back, raise your hands and arms, and take a deep breath. Be grateful.
12. Relax, say thank you to the Sun, offer namaste, and breathe easily. Thank everyone, friends, family, teachers, and nature, for being the beacon and standing shoulder to shoulder to bring you to this moment.

The old bear goes silent and stares at the sky. There goes again, a celestial wanderer, Bantu, to his new destination, a new world Sanjeevani. The Sun spin is a beautiful ritual to practice. It brings you vitality, hope, and gratitude to the beginning, humility, and balance to the journey, and helps you find infinite love and compassion everywhere you go.

Sita Maha Lakshmi

I am a beloved. Relatively, I am beloved by everyone I know. If I must give a name to myself, I will go by Sita Maha Lakshmi. If I must give a name to the world I live in, I call it Sanjeevani. Our ancestors are explorers of the sky. A celestial wanderer blessed them to make a little world of their own. Be it our universe, our world, our home. In return, our ancestors sacrificed their starships, pledging to stay at home. The philosophy is similar to humans' "***Vasudika Kutumba***," strengthening into one family.

I cannot reveal much; I mean how we look and sound, all of that.

I heard many stories about humans. Give humans a little bit of something, a little something; they will figure it all out, one step at a time. It is only safe to give more details if there comes a day when we must merge our worlds and see the same Sun. When that day comes, we will reveal to each other.

But this is about something other than what I cannot share but what I can.

Sanjeevani is a pretty flower, a blush of shiny pink starlight smudging a billion-petal pink lotus with gold dust.

And we have a very naughty guest.

Sun spin always makes him hungry. Always.

As soon as he arrives, Bantu launches into a nearby Banana field, hopping with his tail, feet burning with heat, and a hungry stomach.

One little monkey in a banana field realizes he cannot eat all bananas all at once, and a memory of a celestial bee reminds him he can. It takes a little while to lose his stellar memory.

So, one monkey becomes many monkeys, and soon, an entire army of monkeys invades a beautiful banana field to satisfy the hunger of a sky traveler.

Birds of Sanjeevani sang their hearts out; natives recognize this as the most festive. We all got a little optimistic and curious, smiling ear to ear and wondering what could be now.

However, to our disappointment, we quickly found the banana field laying waste, and our harvest is now in trade to an unknown beneficiary.

Drum rolls and guard bird Garuda brought us to a gathering.

My beloved father, the chief of our land, gave summons and assurances very quickly. He sent Garuda, the guard bird, to find the culprit.

I, however, couldn't help but curiously recognize the minutiae of the happenings. Birds have a happy song; unripe fruits are untouched, and all the sweet fruits are gone.

"Who else can make up a storm out of thin air?"

"Bantu?"

"Is he here?"

I ran across the farm, tracing him foot by foot, but I found my way back to a stone in every possible way. It's a shining blue stone, Nilam, Sapphire, a precious jewel coated with gold dust. I touched, rubbed, and saved it in my palms and quietly departed from the fields.

Garuda: A Celestial Eagle
Nilam: A Sapphire Gemstone

Sanjeevani nights are the most beautiful; we have two moons, one a crescent and one full moon, saving us from the darkness. We cannot survive complete darkness. The night sky brings about a billion stars. Our stars glow all gold in warm light. Our nights have glow falls. Glow bubbles light up our nights with a bit of spark all night and disappear under the Sun. Here and there, we rarely spot stars of tiny red, pink, green, blue, and purple. Before sleep, we all gather to see the stars together, gaze at them for a long time, and hear one good story under the stars about other worlds. It is crucial to know that we are not here alone; there are many worlds, many wanderers, many species, and many good neighbors.

Everyone went to sleep. I picked up Nilam and rubbed it a little, shining blue and gold dust at midnight. I quietly held it, rubbing it a little, "Bantu, I am Sita; you are safe now, you can wake up."

The stone slowly became mushy. So, I dropped it on the ground. Wobbling, stretching, and then grabbing the rocks next to it, the blue stone woke up to a Mountain and slowly became a Monkey.

Garland of golden stars across the neck, blue skin, stars dust glimmering all over the body, eyes wide, ears wide, crescent moon amid the golden dust on the forehead, long fiery orange dust tail.

"I am home." He said, looking into my eyes enthusiastically, spreading warmth, and loosening up after a long nap.

I quickly commanded, "**Shrink into the size of a tiny little bee.**"

"Garuda is keeping the watch."

Bantu dropped his size to a minuscule, and I picked him up and asked,

"Did you eat all the bananas."

He nodded, and his eyes almost said you can't be angry with me.

"I am thirsty," Bantu spoke.

"Let me take you to the river."

A few steps towards the river, Garuda caught me. Of course, the celestial bee cleverly took the flight away.

"This is not the time to go to a river; kindly return home."

"I am thirsty, and I need river water."

"Let me get you something, he rushed and brought me back the leaves of Tulsi."

"Now, don't give this old bird a tough time; go back to your cottage and drink some water with these leaves." He advised.

I said "Yes" and took a return to my cottage.

I put the leaves in the mud pot and gave it to Bantu.

He drank and burped.

I sighed with relief.

"Why are you here, troublemaker and treasure seeker?" I asked.

He said, "I miss you and want to be with you."

"Well, aren't you supposed to find treasures and meet your friend, your chief?"

"Staying away from you feels like staying away from him, too."

"You are home to me now; staying next to you feels like being close to him. "I sighed.

"Listen, you have just recovered me from a treasure."

"How?"

"The bluestone you picked up and called a life out is a treasure."

I rolled my eyes and said, "Isn't it obvious to find a special stone and think of it as a celestial."

"It is, however, for knowing it to be true and having enough faith to call a stone back into life is a treasure; faith is a precious treasure."

"So many stones are lying out there; Very few recognize them as unique, and very few gather the courage to call the stone back to life. But you cared enough to bring me back to life."

I went quiet with an understanding of what Bantu had just said.

"One more thing, I am a clever troublemaker, but you are the treasure seeker here," said Bantu.

"How many treasures are left?"

"How long will it take to find all of them?"

"What if it takes my entire lifetime to find you all the treasures?"

One question after one, I gave him away all my every concern.

Wise wanderers say, "Be on the path; while you are on it, stay close to the ones who make you feel at home."

Saying that, he fell asleep innocently and quietly, wrapping himself in a grass patch.

When a wise one is sleeping right next to you, it is easy to sleep, and I slept well, wrapping up on the bed of grass under the stars.

So much had already happened before I woke up.

Garuda caught Bantu. The little monkey, Bantu, is hanging upside down to one of the Council of Trees.

The Council of Trees is eight in number; they root and stand in a circle. The trees are wise, creative, and kind; they help with clarity. Natives of Sanjeevani sit in circles around the Council of Trees. My beloved father, Nana, as I lovingly refer to him, stood inside the Council of Trees.

The Council of Trees said, "Say your concerns, we will listen. Ask for advice; we will give it. Make your decisions; we will let you know if it is fair and just."

The chief of natives, my beloved father, gave his word of appreciation to Garuda. Garuda took off and flew away to the North.

Before the chief of our world could begin addressing and declaring Bantu as the culprit. I hastily ran into the circle of the Council of Trees and held the hand of my beloved father.

Nana gave me that look. "Don't you think you are overstepping here?" I began talking to the Council of Trees.

"The Monkey, Bantu, is a friend of mine, a guest; he isn't aware of the laws of our world. He didn't intend to spoil our farms. Bantu is hungry; he ate all the ripe fruits while sharing them with our birds, leaving unripe fruits untouched; he didn't waste or trade one single fruit; he ate them all by himself."

Nana raised his voice and softly spoke, "How can a monkey eat all the bananas?

"Bantu is a celestial wanderer, my beloved friend; he came Sun spinning and is on a hunger spree. One rule of our land is to feed the hungry; he hasn't asked our permission; if he did, we would have gladly fed him; if I saw him coming, Bantu would have been a guest of honor, but I found him only after he ate the fruit."

The chief nodded in agreement, and the Council of Trees dropped Bantu.

Nana, addressing the natives, spoke, "We are forgiving Bantu for eating the bananas. However, for not asking for permission, we intend to punish him. From today, Bantu offers us Seva. If anyone needs help, call him, ask him for Seva. He will be at your service once the Seva is complete; feed him well. Wanderers come here to bless us. Honor him and take his Seva. If he fails, Sita, on his behalf, will offer Seva."

Natives clapped, cheered, and hailed the judgment. Bantu jumped up and down, did somersaults, dropped to the ground, and slept.

Seva: An act of love.

I, however, found myself walking home with my beloved father advising me. "Remember, a wanderer can never be a friend, can never be family to someone, they are a blessing, they give gifts, but they are not family."

But I haven't asked him for any blessings; he is just a friend.

"Sanjeevani honored many wanderers as guests; they come here to bless us, bring us resources, joy, wellbeing, happiness, and peace. They have always been the guests, never a friend or family."

I walked home alongside my beloved father silently.

My beloved mother, Amma, as I lovingly refer to her, brought me Mangoes to eat. While relishing my fruit, Amma massaged my hair with hibiscus oil and told me in the ear. "If he wants you to be a friend, just be a friend, play with him, smile, share with him, and be with him."

But Nana told me wanderers don't know how to be friends and family.

"It's true; wanderers may not have a home, family, or friend, but they know what home all is about, what family is for, what friendship is; they know it; they give us blessings of home, gardens, friendships, and family. You will be okay if you remain true to who you are. Always remember you have a gift of home, loving family, and friendship. So, share the gift of family, friendship, and home with him."

Sanjeevani Sunrises are very festive. Birds sing beautiful songs in the early twilight through the golden light. The birds sing a blessing, give us the weather forecast, watch our sky, keep an eye on passing by wanderers, and say what we can pray for. They also say what trees need water, what fields need little care, what gardens to tend, what fruits and flowers are to smell and taste, what we can expect from the day, small gossip, confessions of the natives, they sing to bring us joy, inspiration, fulfillment, and happenings of Sanjeevani.

Devas feed our world's birds, horses, deer, little fishes, cows, sheep, chickens, ducks, and squirrels. Devi offers prayers with many flowers, herbs, fruits, fire, water, grass, mud, and hymns.

Once the Sun rises, we all gather under the morning Sun to Sunbathe and stretch. There are many rivers to swim in, pools to have private baths, and musicians playing instruments. Once everyone is up and takes the Sun's warmth, natives walk miles to eat the fruits and smell the flowers.

Everyone has a chore to attend markets, fields, and farms, sailing in the rivers, counting resources, teaching, sharing, strengthening skills, sculpting, building, weaving, cooking, caretaking, healing, learning about the world, and some Seva. In the Sun's zenith, we have grand luncheons near the Council of Trees and nap in our gardens. Afternoons, we are easy; we put up with some slow, creative chores; we tend to our gardens, close the markets, clean the pathways, make flower arrangements on every path, around our cottages, drink herbs, eat fruits, take quick baths, gather to see the Sunset, dance, sing, share stories, ask for advice, listen to each other, watch the Sun go down, and gaze at the stars.

Once the stars put up with the show, we cheer and clap, find our way back to our cottages and gardens, share our time and warmth with our family, tend to them, eat a quick dinner, and sleep very well.

Devas: Masculine
Devi's: Feminine

Bantu, however, took giant leaps and bounces to be at peace with the natives of Sanjeevani. He found himself to be everything and be everywhere all at once. Bantu is up with birds and sits with them; birds fly away to another tree. He caught up with Devi as an escort; they drove him away. He tried to befriend Devas as a bird and animal feeder, but the animals fled in fear. In the Sunrise gathering, everyone looked very uncomfortable when Bantu was around. During lunch, they asked me to take him away. Midafternoon, he stood far away gazing at the natives, sitting in groups, and participating in the creative chores. He then tried to be friends with cows, chickens, deer, and ducks, but they weren't interested. During the Sunset gathering, he tried to dance, but no one clapped or cheered. He then tried to tell a story, but not one in the world of Sanjeevani are listening.

Before night, natives petitioned the Council of Trees; "Sanjeevani need protection; wanderers may influence anyone to leave their family and travel with them."

Before the chief can address the petition, a bluebird comes and whispers in his ears, "You have to protect your beloved daughter; I heard she took a celestial trip with Bantu."

The chief quietly gave his consent.

The Council of Trees gave consent to our chief's judgment. "Call upon the spider and weave a web of protection around our world."

The mighty, proud spider slowly walked poignantly toward the Council of Trees. "It will take an entire night for me to weave a web. No one else can cross over our world. Our world, our family, will be protected as one." Said the spider, clasping its feet and walking away regal.

Nana asked everyone to sleep in peace; everyone left with a smile of assurance to their cottage.

My beloved family, however, embraced Bantu with warmth; my mother fed him with fresh fruits, my brother cherished him as a new friend, and my father snuggled him on his forehead.

I took him for a walk in the moonlight into the jasmine field.

Bantu is very silent, a little lost, tiptoeing all along. The full moon is shining all over the field. I turned to the Bantu and said, "Let's play a game."

"What are we playing?" He got all alert, curious, and steady.

"I will pluck the jasmine flowers and drop them wherever I wish to. You must catch them, tend to the little jasmine flowers with care, very lightly, just like a feather, without holding them too much or dropping them to ground, you must care for them very gently."

"My mother nurtured this jasmine garden with the utmost care, and now the jasmine garden is in full bloom. We must give her the flowers, and she will make garlands for us."

Bantu stood erect, ready for the play.

"**Bantu, it's time to be light as a feather,"** I called out loud, plucked a flower, and threw it in the air.

One flower at a time, in every way possible, I have thrown them into the air. Bantu jumping, balancing, rolling, spinning, lazily vaulting, climbing, dropping, and crawling tenderly caught every flower and put it in a sack with good cheer. I smiled at him. "You just started; we have an entire garden to play in."

It took us many loud laughs, running, and windfalls to gather a sack of flowers with his tiny little palms.

We put the sack next to us and laid our backs to the ground on the full moon. Bantu is pleased. As he gently relaxed, I told him, "Bantu, this world is nurtured by many families; they put a lot of love and care into making this a home for us, a family for us. Many wanderers supported us, and I believe you will, too."

"Oh, you just helped me find another treasure." Bantu rolled up and jumped with joy. "A Jasmine Flower?" I questioned.

"Yes, to be a friend, to be a family to someone means you must tend to them, be gentle with them, and care for them."

I smiled and sighed. I quickly rolled up, made a small garland of jasmines, and put it around Bantu's neck, saying. "You are a family now, a dear friend to me, a beloved, someone I care for very deeply; welcome home."

We must go back to the cottage, pick up our grass field, and get a restful sleep.

Bantu woke up to the early twilight, quietly listening to the birds chirping and singing a Sunrise hymn. The song said, "Today it might rain a little, and a wanderer is passing by, and we can all pray for new seeds."

Bantu leaped into the air and dragged the wanderer to Sanjeevani. Everyone saw Bantu forcefully pulling a giant bird in the sky. Bantu gleefully announced to the Council of Trees, "This invisible wanderer is my old friend."

The bird looked very frightened. Wanderers stay invisible. Wanderers don't like to be seen, heard, and cherished. Natives gather quickly around the Council of Trees to see a giant bird with many colors; it looks like a parrot but is very massive. The big parrot became very uncomfortable with all the attention.

Trying to comfort him, Bantu spoke, "Don't be afraid. They are my family. Now go quickly and drop a bounty of seeds across the world."

The big parrot flew across the skies, dropping seeds on its way. Bantu felt an impressive pride; he sensed the natives were very impressed. The parrot bid goodbyes to his friend Bantu and faded out of the world.

Bantu silently, at a distance, escorted Devi to the temple and quietly sat in the prayers. Once the prayers were complete, he ate what they offered to eat.

He sat with natives to watch the Sunrise and then went for a long walk with my beloved father. Once home, he helped my most beloved mother with her jasmine garlands. Just before the deer woke me up, he came running to me. He woke me up by driving the deer away, patting my head, and looking into my eyes with so much love. I sluggishly said, "We have an entire day to ourselves."

Bantu came to the river to drink water with me; we then went for long hikes to find seasonal fruits to eat. I went to take a shower in the private pool, and the Bantu went for a swim in the river.

While I made the flower arrangements on the pathways of Sanjeevani, Bantu realized he must do something all by himself. He quickly remembers the banana farm lying waste to the ground. He went to the farm to clean the debris and prepare the soil by carefully maneuvering and moistening it. Ear to ear, word spread, and everyone came to cheer Bantu for his Seva. I went to see the farm with joy. I told it in his ear, **"See, it's always in your control; everyone likes you, and everyone trusts you."**

In the zenith hour, he sat to eat at the grand luncheon; in the evening, he gave good wise company to my beloved brother, being his cheerful playmate and partner in every stride, giving him inspiring ideas to trade and multiply the joy of living. Bantu finds his way back to me, tending to the flower gardens and plucking flowers into a basket, and in the Sunset gathering, he made many friends to play with, laugh with, hold hands with, and gossip with.

Bantu is the storyteller. In every tale Bantu tells his adventures and praises his chief; he dances and taps along with the natives and makes funny faces, bringing us heartfelt laughter with his quirkiness.

At night, he eats food with my family: my beloved father, my most beloved mother, and my beloved little brother, his beloved family now.

In the sleep, he finds his patch of green field closer to my grass patch. We sleep in the grass gazing at the stars. For being his faithful friend and family, I get to be part of his world, too. I can see the skies as he does, the wanderers flying, our neighboring worlds, star showers, and stars beyond stars; some nights, we receive unexpected guests, wanderers visit Bantu, and I get to be in their friend group.

Ever since Bantu came to Sanjeevani, everything just became better. It's just a better experience of life. Bantu is my family, everyone's family; he is a good friend to everyone, family to every family. There is more laughter in our Sunset gatherings, more feet moving to dance, more voices joining for a chorus, more peace in our early morning gatherings, birds coming from other worlds, and more joy in everyone's home. I have in him an escort, a good friend, someone I can trust, my family, someone I can tend to with loving kindness. I can't help but appreciate him every single day. I told him.

"Bantu, you are special; you can create for us with bare hands, dust, stardust, gold rain, water, birds, and magic."

Since that day, Bantu has become very ambitious; he is always looking to redo a garden, go beyond the world, find wanderers, bring them down to our world, and make Sanjeevani a better place to experience life. He is helping someone heal, making someone laugh, rebuilding a cottage, farming, helping everyone, and distancing himself from me.

Bantus became family to everyone; there was always a group of natives, birds, and trees. Everyone longs to spend time with him, and I miss having him for myself. It gets frustrating that I must share him with everyone else. These are times I fear that he is a wanderer; one day, he will leave me, and I will miss him.

One early morning, I couldn't find him in the world of Sanjeevani. He didn't wake me. Routing from one native to another, I asked every native, every tree, and every bird, and everyone said, "I just saw him; he must be somewhere around." Bantu didn't show up to the lunch, he didn't come by Sunset, the stars showed up in billions, and my eyes tried to find the sky wanderer in light. In my mere existence, I cannot go beyond my world to find someone who didn't promise to return, who didn't say goodbye, but I chose to wait that night. It's just that faith that this is family, and he will return home.

Bantu found him hanging upside down to the Council of Trees early in the morning. Garuda, the guard, brought him to the Council of Trees. Everyone gathered around him; I was relieved that he was there.

Everyone asked, "Where have you been? Sita is up all night and waiting for you to come home."

Bantu looked at me in the eyes, and I looked at him angrily.

You promised to be family. Family means watching the Sunrise and Sunset together. Family means asking permission to leave and telling them when you will return. Family means knowing that everything that happens to you will affect someone else.

Bantu spoke, "I am sorry, I haven't crossed the world. I am just around and was in pursuit of some treasure."

The Council of Trees dropped him to the ground. The chief of our natives, my beloved father, Baba, said, "The Council of Trees decided that Sita must determine the punishment for Bantu.

"Tie a bell to his tail. Everyone who rings the bell can ask something from Bantu."

"Bantu, you must fulfill everyone's desire," I commanded.

Cheering and clapping, natives tied the bells to the Bantu's tails. Natives rang the bell and said many desires in Bantu's ears. They all have countless desires.

"Milk ponds, lotus ponds, oceans, mountains, forests, wildlife, elephants, horses, rainbows, waterfalls, flower gardens, more vegetation, seeds, harvest, butterflies, new recipes, new farms, and cattle.

Gift of inspiring ideas, clarity, wisdom, inner knowledge, faith, trust, and loyalty. An abundance of resources, minerals, renewed energy, wealth for many generations, gold, diamonds, emeralds, rubies, corals, pearls, sapphires, and many precious stones.

Rebuild our cottages as mansions with good ventilation, beautiful gardens, ponds, blessed spaces, and natives living in them with Presence of mind, pleasant hearts, compassionate smiles, togetherness, affection, right actions, and pious intentions.

Birds can sing songs with blessings of protection, fulfillment, victory, joy, love, harmony, and affection.

Re-architect our golden temples with flower creepers, beautiful assemblies, bring auspicious occasions, and gratitude to recognize and celebrate everything and everyone.

Hymns to liberate us, reduce our anxieties, strengthen our souls, clear our obstacles, and destroy our fears."

Bantu heard all of them, twisting, twirling, dropping to the ground, and stretching sluggishly.

He showed us the stone. "Cinnabar, this could be a treasure. This precious stone will fulfill all your desires."

I quickly said, "If you say it is a treasure, it is a treasure."

Bantu looked at me and said, "You don't understand, do you?"

I looked at him and said, "Well, then explain."

"You can recognize its value and elevate this cinnabar to its worth. It is something in you, your power, and your heart creating value for it, making it a unique treasure."

"Someone must look at this stone with a certainty of significance to realize its value, elevate it to its worth, and become a treasure."

He kept the cinnabar in my hand, saying, "You recovered many treasures; you know how to recover this, too." I held the cinnabar in a tight grasp.

In the Sunset gathering, a male bird started to sing. We are all a little taken back by the fortune teller. Because it is the only bird of its kind, it was always lonely and never sung. It is the first time it has Sung; the song is deep and has a message. "Our little world is changing; we have new desires and must find a new Sun, moon, life, and friends to make this place home again. Tomorrow's Sun won't be bright enough for us to live a good life."

Natives became anxious; my beloved father gave herbs to bring relief and calmness to the atmosphere. The Council of Trees said, "We have everything it takes to have a good life; we must find a Sun."

I have commanded Bantu, "**Become as tall as a mountain or more than that, grow taller, beyond the world, but find us another Sun.**"

Bantu became taller and taller. "I can see the Sun from the golden mountains. We may merge our worlds."

"The golden mountains?" questioned my beloved father.

"Yes, there are waterfalls, wildlife, living in golden mountains, it has vast oceans." "Wildlife and us?"

"I lived with them; they are my family. Sita came to visit us. I will be the mediator and help create good boundaries; it's a Promise," said Bantu.

"We don't have starships; if we start exploring now, we will all become explorers again, and this will disturb life in our world." said the chief of Sanjeevani, my beloved father.

Natives are dismayed and hurt that what we have tended to, nurtured too, will disappear; just in one night, this world can disappear.

So many discussions, and the chief listened patiently to them and decided to merge our worlds.

I, however, looked at my palms; the cinnabar spread its red into my palms, imprinting a stamp of a glowing red Sun.

I raised and opened my palms to show the assembly of natives. It filled the atmosphere with enthusiasm and hope. It's a shining Sun in my palms. Bantu leaped into the air and brought loads of cinnabar, tattooed Sun on every native's palm.

"This is a treasure of hope, empowerment, and good inspiration to make things possible; take the next step, trusting, hoping empowerment leads to a beautiful destination."

"But we don't have starships; we sacrificed all of them." The chief of Sanjeevani reminded us.

"Well, we will have to make one now." Advised the Council of Trees.

"How?" asked the chief.

"It's all about finding the one willing to hold and move our world."

Everyone looked at each other, and a Turtle enthusiastically came forward. "I am good at this; I love to go around our world; I see and know our world layer by layer, and I am slow and steady. I can hold it better."

I said, "Yes."

A Turtle? We must go there as fast as we can.

Yes, it's only the Turtle who can take us to the Sun.

"How?" asked my beloved father.

The Turtle walked every inch of our world and lived longer than anyone who lived here, and if there is someone who invites the Sun into our world every day, it is the Turtle, he is aware of our clan by many generations.

It's an uncharted territory; the Turtle must become more familiar with the skies.

That is the very reason we must create our path, trust that help is all around us, and take steps toward it. This journey will help us grow and strengthen enough to receive the new Sun. We must do this all by ourselves, trusting each other to be a family. It feels lonely, but we all have each other. There will be many pathways to explore, but we are explorers. We are going home; we must walk our way home with all we are.

I looked at Bantu and said, "You inspired me to create my own path and walk alongside you to find the invisible mountain."

"Aha."

But the natives are not convinced. They ask for a competition between the Bantu and the Turtle. Let them first go around the world and see who comes first.

The little celestial monkey Bantu and the homebound Turtle stood at the edge of our world.

Bantu turned to Turtle, saying, "Be aware, trust your heart, and go steady like you always do."

"Of course. I got it." Said the Turtle.

Bantu took his usual twelve-step routine to fly around our world, and the Turtle took his next step into the unknown.

We all eagerly awaited with so much silence. But within very few moments, the Turtle came first, and Bantu came next.

Everyone cheered.

"It only took two small steps for me to go around our world." Proudly spoke the Turtle, almost flying in the air.

"Turtle is the starship, the Turtle is the treasure; if you trust yourself with your journey, new pathways and new gateways open to take you where you want to go, and you just have to walk." Said Bantu.

I smiled and said to Bantu. "It is time we recover another treasure." "What is it?" he asked. I went and brought freshly baked pots from fire and gave him a pot filled with river water.

"Lead the ocean to protect our boundaries with this river. These rivers represent who we are and what we are here for; this will help the oceans to recognize us."

"Are you talking about the treasure of giving and receiving?" Bantu questioned me with a smile on his face.

"Yes, what are we if you don't give what we have, and what will we ever be if we don't know how to receive." I smiled back.

Bantu gave a long gaze at the fire cups and the river water.

I commanded "**Bantu, you can go anywhere and obtain anything;**"

"It's time you go first," I said.

"Sunset is happening; we will wait for the moon to lead us on our journey."

Everyone cheered for Bantu. He is gone with the Sun, holding fire cups of water, and we are all waiting for the moon to begin our voyage.

Before he left, he told me in the ear, "Remember this: You are never alone; I will always have an eye on you; you are my beloved family. And remember, you can lead everything back to the Sun. Good luck on your adventure."

Bantu

I am naughty, more like a rebel and less like a cute monkey. I get it, I get it, you know me as a good friend. But I wasn't like this before; I am a troublemaker, a rebel without a cause, curious, intelligent, strong, and good with movements. I move with air, light, fire, water, and dust. I am not just good at it; I am great at making storms out of many elements.

My existence was a nightmare. I can tease you to tears, burn you down to air, make your worst nightmares come true. Many tried to chase, control, or help. But I am gifted with a force and can go beyond everything, galloping parkour, and strength no one could match up with.

My freedom and my existence brought destruction and disturbance to many worlds. No, I wasn't that wanderer looking to bless every world; I am the opposite of that; I am genuinely the opposite of that. I merged species and galaxies, broke constellations, reason for existential crisis, took species to faraway worlds, threatened their survival, hidden galaxies, dragged starships to unknown dimensions, changed the star paths, made storms, drank oceans, and even swallowed the Sun. Everyone who naively trusted me with directions was lost forever. I play like that curiously. I am alone, have a terrible reputation, and no one trusts me, but I am still high in my spirits.

One day, everything in and around me found a delicate stillness. I met my blue prince, commander, chief, and dearest friend.

At first, there is something dark. Out of the darkness came something blue, for every little blue came little glowing yellow. Now the blues want to touch the yellow glow. So, every time the blues and yellows try to connect, the green comes alive. A dust of orange stars brought momentum to this dance. Some red, some purple, out of nowhere came many colors and rainbows. I was watching the grandness of the spectacle; everything in my existence felt the lightning, breathtaking wonder, and the prince came out all by himself on a dozen white horses with an enchanting smile and an effortless presence.

"Who are you?" I asked.

"How special you look;" I embarrassed him as an old friend.

"You are pleasing to my eyes; I want to sing parodies to praise you, take you to every place I have been to, and drop pearls for every word you spoke."

I didn't know until then that someone's presence can somehow elevate you; it did, kindly so.

Before he could answer, I was curious already, jumping from world to world, universe to universe, tired, exhausted, but I couldn't find a match or a resemblance of him.

In every world, every universe, by every axis, view, orbit, and in any dimension, I found him, and he took my breath away.

I did ask him, "What are you made of?"

He smiled, and that smile was haunting.

I found myself in a pinching silence, but his presence brought endearing joy; my blue prince was very pleasing to my eyes, and every word he spoke with loving compassion melted my heart, and I became a dear friend. How could I not?

We became friends, we got to play in stars, galaxies, universes, and worlds, and just like that, I got to go beyond with him and see the creation with him.

He arrives and disappears, arrives, and disappears. To go beyond him, to escape his magnetism, to forget his charismatic presence, and to just be myself became impossible.

Whenever we meet, he has a story to tell, inspires me, and sets me to achieve the mission for him. He says the mission is "***Lokha Kalyanam***". He will politely ask for my help, saying this will benefit the world with well-being, joy, happiness, and prosperity.

Once, I stopped him from leaving me, held him close, embarrassed him, looked into his eyes, and asked, "What must I do to have your presence? Whatever the mission, whoever you want me to rescue, I will. But I must stay in your presence. Always."

He agreed it's an excellent idea; I feel the same, you are very dear to me.

He told me, "Dear friend, wherever you go, find something you love, look at it, touch it, or call me into it. I will appear; this is my promise."

If there is nothing around to make you feel the love, go ahead, and look at yourself with love; I will appear. But if you cannot look at your reflection, if there is only darkness, ask me to be the loving light; I will be a star, a Sun, a moon, I will come to you.

I heard him, trusted him, and with his assurance, I traveled long and far to unknown worlds, uncharted territories, and in every world, every path; I went by his mission to benefit worlds with welfare, happiness, and prosperity.

I can never be my old self again, can never cause pain to anyone, can never trouble anyone; I simply couldn't. I lost my ability to do so.

My movement found its rhythm with the Sun; I came into momentum with his mission to benefit worlds with welfare, happiness, joy, and prosperity. Ear to ear, everyone spread a good word about my good reputation, brought fame to me, and many worlds became my friends, and they trusted me as family. They gave me gifts, praised me, built fine mansions, and served me good food.

Everywhere I go, celebrating like their own, I became a friend, family, and a dear one to everyone. I felt seen, heard, and understood. I told them this change had nothing to do with me but everything to do with him, my dearest friend, chief, and commander.

They will ask, who is it? But in every world, he came to appear different. For a few, I could show a boy; for a few, I could offer a flower and a star. For a few, I could show a stone, a mountain, a butterfly, or a young prince. Everyone said that they understood. But I can clearly say that they still didn't get to see him as I saw him. They didn't get to see him through my eyes. If only they could see him through my eyes, they would have known what a true blessing it is to find him and to offer seva to him.

So, the easy way to give out his essence to the world is to tell them about our good friendship, an endearing friendship that brings happiness to mine and many hearts.

I led an army for his mission and led them in the spirit of spreading joy, happiness, welfare, and prosperity.

He came to me in every possible way. With him by my side, I went beyond the world, the universe, the light and dark. Like any wanderer, I became wise. I finally understood the more I appreciate, the more I have of him. He is everywhere; even though I didn't ask of him, he is everywhere.

I became one wise wanderer thriving on adventures. Just like that, I got to go beyond all by myself, beyond everything in creation. From beyond, I realized I am. After all, I am living in his world, in his creation; I see what he wants me to see, listen to what he wants me to listen to, meet whom he wants me to meet, and touch what he wants me to feel.

Even if I try, there is nothing that separates me from him. When I understood that, I dropped the act of being a wise wanderer and became a playful child. I gave up on myself; I surrendered willfully and became friends with everyone who found me. Now, that is a story, and it will always be about him, and for you, it will always be the friendship we share.

Now, let's see the live forecast of the journey ahead.

This beautiful Sunset journey from Sanjeevani to the Golden Mountains is short; going there usually takes my twelve-step routine. What is interesting about this journey is I am carrying the river of Sanjeevani in a fire cup. Which means I must go to the Golden Mountains before the Sun Sets.

The fire will perish once the Sun is down, and the river will flow out of my hands. If I use force and speed up, the fire will rise to a firestorm, and the river will dry up.

I have been a celestial bee for a while now; I got my learnings; we don't get to use tricks and traps and ask for help while taking these journeys. We go there one step at a time, watching our surroundings and moving forward to the destination without any delays or distractions.

Wanderers always go North. I turned North, looking at the Sun, and took one step at a time, finding my momentum with the force of the Sun, not too slow or fast, just about alignment with the Sun's momentum. I have already come to the Golden Mountains.

I quickly dropped the river water into the ocean. I was watching the sea find its momentum with the river.

In Sanjeevani, as the Sun goes down, everyone celebrates the Sunset, honoring the Turtle and preparing themselves to sleep. The chief of the land gave herbs to help them sleep well. The Council of Trees blessed the Turtle and delivered a message to him. "Keep your fins free and fly. We will be awake and watching over you."

The natives brought milk, honey, flowers, fragrances, oils, water, mud, and herbs. They cleaned the Turtle, played the drums, and decorated the Turtle. They tapped on the Turtle's tail, the Turtle's shell, then the neck of the Turtle. From tail to crown, they were tapping every inch of the Turtle to tune its life into a starship. Butterflies came and cleaned the eyes of the Turtle. They told him in the ear, "Release everything that is holding you back, go slow and steady, even if it is wobbly, take one step forward."

The chief of Sanjeevani gave the Turtle instructions to the destination. "Look up at our stars; there are four borders to protect our world. Inside them are two circles protecting nine interlocking triangles, four pointing up and five pointing down. When you find the same star path, that is our destination, our home. Until then, slow, and steady, one step forward."

He turned to his beloved daughter and said, "My beloved daughter, we all must go to sleep for the night. I predict you might not sleep tonight; you must be awake. Since you commanded the Turtle to be a starship, you must witness his journey; remember this: you are not alone. Whether it gets lonely or dark, you are at home, and we are beside you. We may be asleep, dreaming, but we are right beside you. We love you and will see each other as soon as the Sun is up."

Sita hugged her beloved parents; they were very proud of her.

Sita tapped the Turtle's fins, and the Turtle dropped out of Sanjeevani. It went around the world in circles, and they all gave a final shout-out: "Stick to the east to go home; the Sun shows up."

The Turtle is glowing gold in the dark overlaps to merge with the world of Sanjeevani. They became inseparable. Sanjeevani wrapped up and fitting as a shell of the Turtle glowing as pink clusters; the spider web is spread across the shell, like a golden web. The Council of Trees sent their roots to form a green gear around the shell. The fins, head, and tail are gold, glowing like a star. The Turtle can now only listen to Sita. Sita is sitting in the dark, looking at the terrain of gold, watching the stars, and the Turtle takes the flight.

The ocean found its momentum with the river; the rare blue moon generously rose in the night sky. The family of fish was awake to streak and drive the ocean forward with a blue glowing luminescent. I lead them to spread the seas around the golden mountains.

The rules to drive the oceans are simple: become the ocean. Under the blue moon, I am just a drop of the sea, glowing blue, like every fish, and streaking forward to go around the golden mountains.

As I move forward in high spirits, the first obstacle appears like a mighty mountain, glowing gold at night. Alluring me to lean on, rest a little, eat something for dinner, and sleep. I am very aware that the Golden Mountains do not have any descendants around them. So, I touched it with my fingers. The mighty mountain just became a path, and I went ahead.

A few yards forward, under the enchanting blue moon-friendly stars, the second obstacle came in like a shark. Rising to face me in the eye, with pitiful eyes, she told me, "I have been driving the ocean with all my might; I am starving. Can I feed you? I promise to lead the ocean around the golden mountains."

Before I could say something, it opened its mouth wide, and I had no choice but to take a quick tour into its mouth and quickly detour out of its mouth. The shark dropped itself to the ocean, thinking it fed on me, and fell asleep, sliding away with the waves.

As I lead the blue oceans forward, I can feel my dearest friend, the elephant, waking up to the sound of the ocean waves. As I said, once we call ourselves someone's friend or family, we share our presence with them forever. The herd of elephants stood guarding the golden mountains and keeping a watch on the ocean's way. Their world is changing, and they know it.

The third obstacle came in as a night shadow; the clouds came to wrap around the blue moon, it became very dark, the fish lost their blue glow, and I couldn't find my path forward. I kept my tail growing to reach the clouds and wipe them off the blue moon.

It became to glow, the fishes' stroke with the blue glow, and high spirits. I led them very joyfully.

Sita sat through the night watching the golden terrain and losing herself in the beauty of the unknown. It was dark and lonely; stellar spectacles and many worlds were around. Sita didn't lose herself in any of it; she remained calm, clear, and steady. She is the first one to survive the darkness from Sanjeevani. Slow and steady, one step forward, the Turtle took its final step and came under the star paths. Hanging up in the sky, it asked Sita to confirm if the star's path aligned with Sanjeevani. Sita went around the world, watching the alignment of Sanjeevani with the star paths.

Sita snuggled the Turtle to appreciate their arrival safely. Turtle smiled and said, "Don't hurry; it will take five doorways to merge into the Golden Mountains. Be one world with it to see the Sun."

Sita gently nodded, and the Turtle dropped onto the first doorway.

A golden snake guard woke up with a huge streak. Sita took a massive blow of fire, protecting the Turtle's eyes. With one single shot of fire, Sita fiercely burned to become a bundle of fire, and nothing was left of her except the wilderness of fire.

The snake gave a sneaky smile, an angry one.

Whatever is left of Sita is very little fire; she stood between the Turtle and the snake, keeping up a fight. The snake shot the fire fourteen times, and the little spark of fire grew into wildfire, raining little fire flowers into the world of Sanjeevani.

The fire flowers brought abundant resources, minerals, renewed energy, wealth for many generations, prosperity, vegetation, seeds, harvest, and cattle. Cottages became mansions, lotus ponds, milk ponds, beautiful spaces, structures, golden temples, and assemblies.

Out of the fiercest fire came a bunch of fire butterflies, which became windshields to protect the Turtle's eyes, and the Turtle entered the second doorway. The snake shot ten fire shots, and the ball of fire went around the world to take it all in; if there was something left of Sita, it was only the fire, the raw fire. I could see her fight, giving it all of her and dropping fire flowers to give "Inspiring ideas, clarity, wisdom, inner knowledge, faith, trust, loyalty, presence of mind, pleasant hearts, compassionate smiles, togetherness, affection, right actions, and pious intentions to her world."

The Turtle went into the third doorway. There was not much fire left in the golden snake, but the evil one gave ten more fire shots. The snake keeps up the fight with wildfire against its zeal to protect. The fire flowers brought "Birds that can sing songs with blessings of protection, fulfillment, victory, joy, love, harmony, and affection."

The Turtle came into the fourth doorway, the golden snake gave away eight fire shots, and the wildfire gave away "Auspicious occasions, and gratitude to recognize and celebrate everything and everyone. Hymns to liberate, increase immunity, reduce anxieties, strengthen the souls, clear obstacles, and destroy fears."

The Turtle came to the final doorway, merging the forests, ocean, golden mountains, and the pink flower of Sanjeevani to align with star paths and become one world. I was standing there with my eyes filled with tears, seeing her burning away. The little fire of her rose and beyond nurturing like a mother, fierce like a protector, and is everywhere around, like beyond.

I reached the Turtle with oceans. The Turtle is sobbing relentlessly; we lost Sita to the fire. The wildfire came alive; it stood still, leaning into me, staring at me, asking if there was anything I could do to bring her back to life, a form, something to come out of this little fire left of her.

The golden snake came back, and before it could shoot any fire, wildfire burned the snake into a garland of lotuses and gave it to me. "A treasure of accomplishment, completing a journey, keeping a promise without fear."

I cried uncontrollably and helplessly without a celestial memory.

Twilight came up, the Sun dust, the moon dust was all around, a few stars were still awake, and a streak of white light came out of nowhere. The wildfire tried to escape the world of Sanjeevani before the Sun showed up. But the spider web didn't allow her to go; after all, it weaved a thread to not let her go.

Once in a blue moon just like that the white light came in like rainbows in full circles, like the rain of pearls dropping, a dozen white horses, and a young prince.

Above and beyond, the wildfire went around him, bursting like fireworks and butterflies, inch by inch, looking at the magnificence, the moon's glow, lotus feet, the decedent of the Sun, with the Nine treasures.

My chief, my blue prince, my commander, and now her beloved stood there still smiling in his ever-enchanting presence.

The little fire beam aligning to his form, in the golden hour, with the very first Sunrise of the new world, she brought herself back to a glowing presence as his reflection, to a new life.

Sita is glowing, golden, enchanting as a belonging to his magnetic presence in his protection. Looking eye to eye, heart to heart, and recognizing each other to be one in soul, sharing same presence.

Her beloved took her palms and stared at the cinnabar spread as the Sun with an endearing smile. He then gave her two mangoes covered with the bees and said, "I heard you love to eat mangoes as soon as the Sun comes up. It's time for us to see the new Sun, these mangoes are sweet enough to attract many bees."

She smiled.

I sat there in enchantment, gleaming and beaming with joy, smiling ear to ear, losing my mind and movement; it's been a while since I saw him, and looking at him one more time is always a pleasure. As I said, it's always worth the wait.

Sita sent bees on my way to tingle, tease, and make me roll and laugh like a child. She looked at him and asked. "Since you brought me back to life, does it mean I exist because you exist?"

He smiled and said politely, "Ah, you can say that, but the truth is the ceaseless fire within you brought me into existence with a new purpose. It's your spirit, that resides in my heart, that decides my path, and that can bring me back to life again and again."

Natives woke up to a grand Sunrise. My blue prince gave a welcome with white cows and coconuts to drink milk, eat fruit, and celebrate the new Sun. Birds sang songs of love. Everyone is happy, celebrating, spreading joy, cheering, and showering them with love, warmth, affection, colors, fire flowers, blessings, and a flower shower.

The gift of a new world, a new Sun, happiness, prosperity, protection, and harmony enchanted me.

Sita's father, mother, brother, friends, and family wrapped her in warmth and affection.

Sita's family thought of him as a rescuer. The Council of Trees thought he was a knight, a descendant of a new world, of the new Sun. The birds thought of him as Sita's beloved. But I knew who he was, and now she is inseparable to his presence, his beloved.

My blue prince, my chief turned to the chief of Sanjeevani, Sita's beloved father, and asked, "With your permission, chief, shall I let loose the spider web? Sanjeevani can blossom and expand itself into the new world."

The chief of Sanjeevani said, "I weaved it for protection."

He spoke politely, "Trust me, she is protected in this world and beyond."

Sita's beloved father, the chief of Sanjeevani, gladly gave permission with a heartful smile.

Her beloved, as they call him now, took a little fire spark on Sita's forehead and blew it into the spider web. The spiderweb left its shackles and became a beautiful landscape holding and standing between the Ocean and Sanjeevani.

I found my movement, jumped into the air, teasing him for the attention. But I can see that my blue prince's attention is into Sita's palm, looking endearingly at the cinnabar imprint of Sun. So, I ran steadfast, to paint myself with the cinnabar and ran back to him, pleading for his attention.

He gave away laughter, rolled his eyes, and hugged me. We jumped into the air, dived together into the ocean to play.

"Finally, you are here; I knew we would meet again; I am so happy to see you" I said, jumping with joy, wrapping myself shyly, and with a wide smile.

"I must; you made some big promises to my beloved Sita, to be her family, to watch every Sunrise and Sunset, in every world and beyond." He smiled.

"I came here as a beloved" he said with a smile.

Elephant

It's a tradition that the story begins and ends with the same voice. I am a great storyteller, but I am also a compassionate listener. Listening to Bantu, Sita, and their adventures gives me great happiness. It inspires me. So, I took my adventure and went on a long terrain to make acquaintance with our new neighbors. After all, we all belong to one world now. As I walked, long and far, trumpeting here and there to let the neighbors know they must expect a guest anytime soon. I finally came to my destination. I met the chief, Sita's father, with a very good smile. He snuggled me with great affection and made announcements to introduce me to his world. It feels like I am home. I watched the Sun rise with my new acquittance, sitting next to my new chief as his pet. I can hear the lion roar from the Golden Mountains as a symbol of earning the right to rise and shine, inviting the Sun to our territory as the new sovereign of Golden Mountains. You know it's true, once you are family to someone, you will always be aware of them, distance doesn't matter.

Note from the Author

I am an introverted, shy girl. If you ever ask me to tell a story, I will gladly give you the beginning, the conflict, and the end of the story. But I have always been a good listener.

My maternal grandfather is a good storyteller, he would tell us bedtime stories every night in the summer holidays. His only rule is that we must continuously nod while listening to the story. I gladly did nod.

My mom told me bedtime stories from the grand Indian Mythology. Like in every Indian household, the story of Ramayana is told in our home too. I have listened to Ramayana and will continue to listen to it all my life. This book draws its origin and inspiration from it. "Jai Sita Ram".

When I read Paulo Choleo's Alchemist, I was hugely inspired. I was just about to graduate, and I found my personal legend. Ever since then signs, omens, synchroneities, self-work, and purpose became my everyday language.

I was sitting under a tree, when I got inspiration to write this book, I wrote one page, and said I am done. I don't have it in me to write more than what I have already written. Three years, and as I finish writing this story, I can say, it didn't take great imagination, intelligence, curiosity, skill, or hard work to write this story. I simply listened to my heart and put together a good story for you to read.

Once you complete reading it, take time to share it with your loved ones too. They will remember you fondly for taking some time to tell them a bedtime story. Sweet Dreams.

Printed in the United States
by Baker & Taylor Publisher Services